W9-AEX-846

In loving memory of Poppa,
David, Olivia, Geordie, Jamie and Kaitlyn

Carter, Anne, 1953-
from Poppa
Text copyright © 1999 by Anne Carter
Illustrations copyright © 1999 by Kasia Charko

Published by
Lobster Press Limited
1250 René-Lévesque Blvd. West, Suite 2200
Montréal, Québec H3B 4W8
Tel. (514) 989-3121 • Fax (514) 989-3168
www.lobsterpress.com

Edited by Jane Pavanel

Canadian Cataloguing in Publication Data

ISBN 1-894222-02-4

I. Charko, Kasia   II. Title

PS8555.A7727F76 1999   jC813'.54   C99-900676-2
PZ7.C24272F76 1999

Printed and bound in Canada

from Poppa

Written by
Anne Carter

Illustrated by
Kasia Charko

Lobster Press Limited

The wind rattled the front door of Poppa's cabin. Marie shivered. Winter was arriving on the lake.

"Do you have to go, Poppa?" Marie asked her grandfather.

"All the leaves have fallen," Poppa answered. The shadows of the bare branches reached through the window and played like fingers in Poppa's white curls. "It's time I head south."

"Like the ducks?" Marie asked, smiling to think of Poppa flapping his arms and flying off like one of his beloved ducks.

"The mallards and the pintails left weeks ago," Poppa said. "Only the wood ducks are still here."

"Why can't you stay this winter?" Marie asked.

For as long as she could remember, Marie had run the long path from her house in town to visit her grandfather in his cedar cabin by the lake. There had never been a winter without Poppa.

"Your mother thinks the cold will be too much for me. She says it's time I turn into a snowbird."

"But I can take care of you," Marie said eagerly. "I'll dig out the path and stack the woodpile for your fire."

Poppa shook his head, wondering out loud, "My little Marie, when did you grow so big?"

He tapped his chest beneath his blue woolly sweater. "No, your mother's right. This heart can't fight the cold of another winter."

"I can take you skating when the lake freezes over," Marie argued. "Remember how warm we get skating across the bumpy ice?"

"I remember," Poppa said, looking at his black skates hanging on a nail by the door. "But these legs won't take me far across the lake this winter."

"Then we'll sit in the ice hut and fish. You'll tell me a story while we wait for a tug on the line."

"I feel a tug right now!" Poppa laughed and stretched his stiff fingers across the worn kitchen table. "These old hands can't drill a hole through the ice anymore."

Marie skated one finger up and down Poppa's big, gnarled knuckles before she asked her last question. "Then who will carve the decoys for next summer?"

Every winter, Poppa carved and painted beautiful wooden ducks called decoys. Every summer, people came to the cabin, hoping to buy one. They said Poppa was a master woodcarver. His decoys were so lifelike, they'd fly off if you didn't keep them inside, shut the doors and close the windows tight.

Poppa wrapped his large hands around the small ones of his granddaughter. "Soon, Marie," he promised, "your hands will be ready."

Poppa stood. "I've been making a special decoy. I need your help to finish him," he said.

Marie followed her grandfather into the workroom at the back of the cabin. Their feet made a narrow path through the wood shavings on the floor. On a bench sat a male duck with a crested head.

"It's a wood duck," Marie exclaimed. "You've never made one before."

"He's the king of the ducks," Poppa said. "In Latin, he's called *Aix sponsa.* That means the promised one."

The duck's dark wings were edged with royal blue and spread like a cloak over his downy white belly. Only his crested head remained unpainted.

Poppa began to rummage through his tools. He found a small curved knife and passed it to Marie. "You take the thick edge off his crown while I prepare the palette for his head," he said.

Marie held the decoy tightly against her chest. As she skimmed the blade carefully through the wood, a few shavings curled onto the floor.

"Good," Poppa murmured. He hummed as he selected tubes from his paint box and squeezed their deep colors onto a cracked china plate. With a master's hand, Poppa colored the decoy's head as black as the night sky, hung a snowy white necklace around the neck, then set the decoy on the bench to dry.

"Your turn," he nodded at Marie.

Using a fine brush and following Poppa's instructions, Marie painted the rainbow of the wood duck's head: bright yellow, vermillion red, iridescent green and blue.

She forgot everything as she worked. The cedar cabin was quiet. Marie painted the last delicate stroke... and blinked. Did the drake's feathers ruffle, ever so slightly? She stared at the decoy. His fiery eyes stared back at her.

Taking the brush, Poppa wrote something across the bird's right wing. Marie bent close, her dark curls beside his white ones, and read, "*from Poppa.*"

"He's a gift," Poppa said, "for you."

Marie pressed her face into Poppa's woolly sweater.

"I'll miss you, Poppa," she whispered.

He wrapped his arms around her, then spoke softly, "He's almost dry. Let's tidy up, then take him down to the lake and see how he looks."

Marie helped Poppa clean the brushes and the china plate. They put away the paints and tools, and at last Poppa said, "He's ready. It's time to go."

Cradling the decoy in her arms, Marie imagined he fluttered with excitement as she stepped into the cold air. She tucked him inside her coat and ran down the path. Maples and birches gave way to sweet-smelling cedars. The sleeves of her coat brushed against the fragrant, feathery boughs as she hurried to the shore.

"Put him out a ways," Poppa directed when he caught up with her.

Marie waded out past the dried marsh grasses and set the decoy gently on the water.

"He looks so real," she said, "like he's ready to take off."

But Poppa was squinting up at the heavy clouds moving in over the lake.

"There's snow coming," he said. "And look!" He pointed to a dark mass that was pouring out of the northern sky. "It's the wood ducks. They're leaving today."

The ducks' approach was swift and steady. The only sound on the lake was the whistle of wing tips beating the air. The ducks flew directly overhead, a majestic parade of bright yellow, vermillion red, iridescent green and blue.

They've come for the decoy, Marie thought. She glanced down to where she'd placed Poppa's gift.

"Poppa!" she cried. "He's gone!"

The decoy was nowhere in sight. Marie ran through the water, not noticing the cold drops that splashed into her boots. Her eyes searched desperately up and down the shore, then over the lake, from one empty wave to another. Not knowing what to do, she walked slowly back to Poppa.

Her voice quivered as she spoke. "I lost him. I lost your gift."

But Poppa was staring at the south end of the lake.

Marie turned her head just in time to see a lone wood duck fly straight up from the waves. As his wings swept the air, a spray of water cascaded down to the surface.

"Hoo-eeek, hoo-eeek," the drake called.

Above, the flock seemed to hover for a moment, as if waiting.

"Hoo-eeek, hoo-eeek," they chorused back. The straggler flapped his wings furiously and joined the tail end of the flock. Marie tugged at Poppa's sleeve. "Poppa … do you think … could it be him?"

The wood ducks picked up speed on the southbound wind.
They became smaller and smaller, finally disappearing
over the horizon.

"I know it's you," she shouted after them.

Marie waved her hands in the air. "Goodbye, decoy!
Goodbye!" she called to the silent sky. Her voice echoed
across the lake. *Goodbye.*

"Thank you, Poppa. He was the best gift ever," Marie said, throwing her arms around her grandfather. "I'll watch for him to come back in the spring. He'll be easy to spot with *from Poppa* on his wing."

"Well, imagine that," Poppa said. A warm smile spread across his face.

It was getting late. Poppa rested one arm around Marie's shoulders and they made their way slowly up the path. Snow began to fall around them, soft and thick. Winter had arrived. When Marie took a last look behind her, the lake, even the woods, had disappeared.

But the sweet smell of the cedars lingered, like a memory, on her coat.